CONTENTS

READ, WRITE, RACE

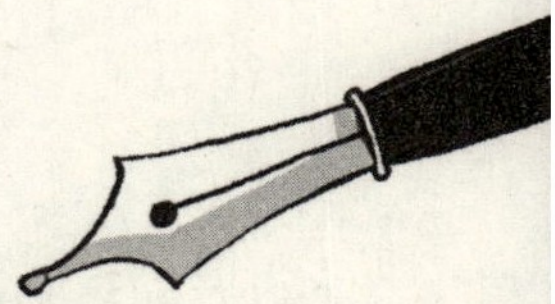

Arti Sonthalia

Illustrated by

Priya Kuriyan

SCHOLASTIC
New York Toronto London Auckland
Sydney New Delhi Hong Kong

Dedicated to
The Lotus Feet of My Guru

Published by Scholastic India Pvt. Ltd.
A subsidiary of Scholastic Inc., New York, 10012 (USA).
Publishers since 1920, with international operations in Canada, Australia, New Zealand, the United Kingdom, India, and Hong Kong.

For information regarding permission, write to:
Scholastic India Pvt. Ltd.
A-27, Ground Floor, Sigma Centre
Infocity-1, Sector 34, Gurgaon-122001 (India)

First edition: July 2022
This reprint edition : February 2026
ISBN-13: 978-93-5471-104-6

Printed in India at Sai Printo Pack Pvt. Ltd.

FIZZLING FIRE

When your ambition ends in disappointment

I, Raghav, sat on the last seat at the back of the classroom. Everyone preferred that I sit there, all my classmates and my teachers too. Even Vedh who had been my best friend since grade one didn't want to sit with me anymore.

He had a new best friend now, Karan.

'Hi Vedh, do you want to sit with me?' I perfectly timed my question as soon as I saw him, before Karan entered the class.

'Ummm ...' Vedh quickly turned around to check if anyone was watching him talking to me.

'No Raghav ...'

'Do you also think ... I am dumb?' I asked Vedh.

'No, of course not.'

I'd known Vedh for a long time, and one thing I knew about him was, he scratched his nose every time he lied. Vedh leaned close and whispered in my ear, 'I want to sit with the more *important* guys this year.' He spotted Karan laughing with his friends. Vedh looked relieved that Karan hadn't noticed him talking to me. He sped away from me like his pants were on fire.

Karan was the *important* guy, and if that wasn't enough to be blessed, I watched every year as he became the teacher's pet.

Karan always came first in maths, English, science and everything that required writing or reading. He had all the latest video games, a closet crammed with toys and a dog that caught Frisbees.

Whatever Karan labelled as cool became the must-have item everyone coaxed their parents to buy them. If he had a new backpack, everyone wanted the same one, and if he had a new haircut, everyone would show up the next day with the same style. And it wasn't long before my former best friend Vedh soon joined Karan's gang.

Vedh had always known that reading and spelling were difficult subjects for me. I remember showing him my last year's paper, completely covered with red marks by Mr Gupta, our teacher. And how I felt like an absolute failure! I'd opened my heart to him, revealed to him my greatest weakness because he was my best friend! Or so *I thought*. But he had teamed up with Karan and the other boys and called me: Dumb! Stupid! And birdbrain! Even after *knowing* I was not dumb!

But this year I was in grade five and I was determined to do my best, to work harder than ever. The only problem was that I had been trying to work hard every day in grade four, grade three, grade two and grade one! But I still saw letters flippy, floppy and wriggly.

Today was the first day of grade five, and I was in my seat at the back of the classroom pasting labels on my neatly covered books. I tried to write my name in my finest handwriting to impress the new teacher. 'RAAGAHV.' Then I wrote my name on the second notebook, 'RAAHGAW.' Then on the third, 'REAGHAVE.'

The neat handwriting built the 'I CAN DO IT' fire inside me just below my belly button and I promised myself, 'Raghav, this is the year you have to prove to everyone that you are not …'

'Hey birdbrain, are you planning to move your desk to the hallway this year?' Karan smirked.

'Look at what he's written!' He laughed loud enough to get everyone's attention.

'He has spelt his name wrong in three different ways!' said Daksh, who was one of the boys in Karan's gang.

I squirmed in my chair. Karan saw me squirm and his laughter grew louder. Now, everyone in class wanted to be by my desk! They were surrounding me and looking at my notebook as if it was on exhibition at The Museum of Curiosities! Even Vedh was there, and that was the hardest blow of them all.

The 'I CAN DO IT' fire in my stomach was fizzling out.

When the others jeered at me, it didn't really matter because I was used to their mocking by now, but when Vedh laughed, it poked my heart like a pin.

I stared at my name spelt in three different ways! How could I have done that? How on earth could someone spell their name wrong in three different ways! No wonder everyone was staring at my notebooks like they were the main attraction at the museum. I was shocked at myself.

'I was just having some fun,' I said, shrugging my shoulders and struggling to laugh with the others.

'That's not fun, that's dumb!' Karan said. 'Don't you know who our teacher is this year?' Karan

spoke as if he were a genius and knew all the answers in the world.

'No.' I tried to speak confidently.

'It's Ms Joseph!' Karan whispered with awe as if he had just announced that Ms Hitler would be leading the class.

'Ms Joseph!' Vedh and the others gasped as if she really was Hitler!

'She is the strictest teacher in the entire junior school,' Karan added. 'If a student doesn't perform well in her class, she makes them stand outside the class for weeks and sends them to the principal's office!'

'Yes! That's true,' Daksh added. Even if it wasn't true, Daksh agreed to everything Karan said.

'So?' I said, trying to act brave.

'So Mr Genius, you might as well move your desk outside now!' And he laughed so loud that Vedh and everyone joined him again. I think Karan's most unique talent was to find anything to make me feel like the tiniest ant in the universe and in return he would be the biggest woolly mammoth!

I imagined myself standing outside F-O-R-E-V-E-R.

The 'I CAN DO IT' fire, the promise of trying harder was stone cold now and, suddenly, my excitement about working hard felt worthless.

I was reminded of a desert. However hard you tried watering the dry sand, nothing would ever grow there. The desert would always be dry and thirsty like me.

ATOM BOMBS

Causing damage through heat and blasts

A lady with jet-black hair tied neatly in a bun entered the classroom. Unlike other teachers who wore salwar suits, she wore a crisp white shirt and black pants.

She stood in the centre of the class as her black eyes scanned us all. From my seat at the back, I watched everyone shrink into their seats. We all looked tiny and meek.

At her first eagle-eyed sweep of the room, the chattering stopped. In her second X-ray scan, everyone quickly settled in their seats. She had not said a word. It was her eyes that were doing all of the work. And in the third thunderbolt look, there was pin-drop silence. Vedh's pencil dropped but he was so scared he didn't even pick it up.

That's when I realized there was truth in what Karan had said: Ms Joseph was Hitler! And if not Hitler—if reincarnation was real—then at least some part of him was reborn in her!

'Hello, fifth graders, I am your new teacher, Ms Joseph,' she said loud and clear. We all shrank deeper into our seats.

'Before I begin with the rules of my classes, I want to introduce you to a new student who has joined our school.' Ms Joseph signalled to someone at the door.

A wheelchair rolled into class. A small, pony-tailed, brown-eyed girl rolled her chair expertly into the room and stopped near Ms Joseph.

Everyone stared at her as if they had never seen someone in a wheelchair before!

'Would you please introduce yourself to the class?' Ms Joseph told her.

'My name is Simran and I love reading,' she said.

'Why are you in a wheelchair?' Karan asked.

Ms Joseph shot Karan a look of disappointment.

'Umm ... I h-hurt myself. Actually, I am not going to be in this wheelchair forever. It's just a matter of a few weeks,' Simran replied confidently.

And I instantly liked her confidence.

'Okay, Simran, please settle down at the back of the class so that you have space and can move in and out of the room easily,' Ms Joseph said kindly.

Ms Joseph pointed a finger at my direction. 'What's your name?' I looked around hoping she was not talking to me.

'You, yes, you. At the back.' This time I was sure it was me.

'Me, it's … it's R-Raghav,' I stammered and everyone laughed.

Her piercing eyes made everyone quiet again.

'Raghav, please move aside the chair from the desk next to you and make space for Simran,' she ordered.

I quickly stood up and nearly stumbled over the chair. Everyone giggled again at my clumsiness. Her eyes widened even more as her X-ray vision swept over everyone in the room.

After I finished making space for the girl in the wheelchair, she settled right next to me. It felt funny to have someone sit next to me, as I was

so used to sitting by myself. I was known as the boy who always sat alone. As soon as Simran got an opportunity, I was sure she too would change her seat.

'I would like everyone to introduce themselves to me and say one line about yourself,' Ms Joseph said.

'Only one line?' Karan asked, as if he could write a biography about himself.

Ms Joseph stared and Karan was quiet.

'I am Vedh and I like to play video games.'

'I am Karan and I am good at all sports. And I have been the best student in all my grades.'

'One sentence, Karan,' Ms Joseph said sharply.

'I am Daksh and, just like Karan, I like to do everything.' Daksh was Karan's parrot.

'I am Neetu. I like reading,' the girl who hardly spoke in class, said very softly.

'She also likes to always be quiet,' Karan said, laughing. But Ms Joseph didn't find it amusing, so he stopped laughing.

After everyone's introductions, Ms Joseph announced, 'Okay class, my first focus for this year is going to be on your reading.'

'Noooo,' I thought to myself.

'Yessss,' The girl on the wheelchair said softly, wiggling with enthusiasm.

Ms Joseph pulled out a lengthy strip of paper, with a long list of words on it. 'I am putting up this list of books I have chosen for you. Every year I put up a new list with a few new books. I'm always looking for exceptionally good books to add to this list. This year, I think you will be pleased with this new selection.'

Added more books! WHY? I thought. Not that I didn't like books but I just couldn't read them. And the harder I tried to read, the more I got frustrated. It was like trying to find a key to a lock and with each key that doesn't fit, your disappointment grows.

'Fantastic!' Simran whispered again with excitement.

'You must read one book a week, out of the ones on this sheet, and every Monday morning, your review report of the book should be on my desk,' her voice thundered as she pinned the sheet on the sideboard.

'I'm sunk,' I thought. My dream of performing better was falling apart, my eyeballs stuck out at the list. Then I looked at Simran's beaming face.

'This is the best class I have ever been to!' Simran cheered.

'Next, spellings are very important. We shall pay special attention to how we write. Each week, I will give a spelling test and I don't want anyone from my class lagging behind.' Ms Joseph peered at each one of us in the eye as if she wanted her words to pierce into our heads.

I felt dizzy. I felt like running out of the class, onto the sports field, to the running track's starting line where our sports teacher, Mr Bolt, could scream 'GO'! And I would run, because that was the only thing I was good at. I would run away from everything, from grade five, from Karan, from Ms Joseph's spelling and reading demands, and most especially, from Simran's thrilled face.

NAME: RAAGAHV
ROLL NO:
CLASS:
SCHOOL:

'I am giving out a comprehension sheet. I want to get an idea of your understanding level and standard of work.' Each word that came out from her mouth was like a military man bombing his enemy's camps one by one. And here, I was the enemy!

'And … NO fooling around,' she said.

But I was not fooling around, I was trying! And now, yet another teacher was soon going to get sick of me, another year I would spend standing outside the class, and another year where I would feel like a piece of trash.

Ms Joseph handed out the sheets. 'Neat work always counts.'

As soon as she reached my table to hand over the worksheet, I asked her, 'Ma'am, please may I use the bathroom?' I had a plan.

Her flashing eyes observed me closely. And then in the sternest voice I had ever heard she said, 'I have been a teacher for twenty years and I know when a boy actually needs to use the bathroom. Now take the assignment and quickly complete it.'

'But, it's ... it's an emergency.' I tried to bring up the urgent face look.

Karan giggled with his mouth covered.

Ms Joseph's face turned to stone.

'First and last time,' she said.

'Thank you, ma'am,' I said and ran out as fast as I could before she changed her mind.

I gave a sigh of relief; if the expression, you never get a second chance to make a first impression was true, then I had saved myself this time!

I spent sometime in the bathroom, turning on and off the faucet, checking in the mirror, trying to flatten my cowlick, walking in the exact centre of each tile, taking care not to step on the cracks because I didn't want to break my mother's back! And just five minutes before class ended, I walked in confidently, feeling as if I had conquered the comprehension sheet.

Ms Joseph was collecting worksheets from everybody. I had never felt gladder.

'So, all of you have submitted your work except …' she looked at me with the look teachers give when they are going to throw an atom bomb, 'Raghav.'

My relief turned into the suffocation you feel just before a storm. I could see it coming.

'Raghav, you will take this worksheet and one more from my desk, finish both at home and show them to me tomorrow morning, others please complete your homework too. Ms Joseph said with a smile that wasn't meant to be a real smile.

What! Two sheets! I wouldn't even be able to do one!

'But … but …' I tried to say.

Ms Joseph's eyes said it all. I knew there was no use arguing. I picked up the worksheets and pushed them deep into my bag, deeper than the deepest part of the ocean, which is the Mariana

Trench. The girl on the wheelchair looked at me and rolled her eyes.

There went my first impression with everybody.

CHEETAH OR SLOTH?

CHEETAH: Fastest animal in the world

SLOTH: Slowest animal in the world

'KA-BOOM! KA-BOOM!' Shlok, my younger brother, roared as he made his dinosaurs go to war, which he did every single evening.

'Shlok, I can't concentrate on my homework! Please lower your voice,' I said, already feeling miserable at the thought of doing not one, but two comprehension sheets.

'But I AM NOT YELLING! The fire-breathing dinosaurs are yelling! They are at WAR! KA-BOOM! The Spinosaurus just won't leave T-Rex today, because the prince stole his gold! He is furious and is going to burn down the entire kingdom. BA-BAM! HISS!' Shlok carried on. He was having a great time in his make-believe world.

'But Shlok, I really can't focus' I said, wishing one of Shlok's wooden dinosaurs would come to life and breathe fire on my homework. It would have been so satisfying to see my sheet burn off!

Then I could tell Ms Joseph that my brother's pet burned it. It seemed like a great solution to my troubles, except for the fact that Shlok didn't have a real dino pet which spat fire!

'Raghav, my Spinosaurus will calm down only on the condition that Prince Raghav plays with Prince Shlok and teaches him all the tricks which Prince Raghav knows best,' Prince Shlok said.

I smiled at the thought of play and at Shlok's innocence, BUT if I played with Shlok, who would do my homework? Instantly, my smile vanished. I looked at the comprehension passage; wriggly twirling letters filled the page. If only I could turn into a dino, I myself would spit fire and burn my homework!

'Are you done with your homework, Raghav?' Mom asked as she came into our room, which was cluttered with Shlok's dinos and other toys.

Done? I hadn't even started. My eyes were just starting to adjust to the glare of the letters.

'I am starting now,' I said.

'Starting now?' I noticed as Mom's eyebrow's curled and her face stiffened.

'I'll finish it, Mom,' I said in my most persuasive voice.

'When will you finish it, Raghav? I don't want you to be fooling around like last year.'

Mom's words spat fire like Prince Shlok's dinosaurs and this time I was burning inside, because I was not fooling around! I was doing my very best! Why couldn't anyone see how hard I tried!

My Mom didn't understand, my first-grade teacher didn't understand, not even my second-grade teacher, neither third, nor fourth and, as for Ms Joseph, I was positive she would never be able to see how much I struggled! If there was one thing I was not doing, it was NOT fooling around!

'Will you please show me what you have for homework?' she asked.

I handed her the sheet I was thinking of starting to work on. I didn't mention the second sheet that was hidden safely in my bag. She would freak out and that would be reason enough for me to sit at my desk till midnight.

Mom took the paper and read. 'Hmm… it's a passage on the melting of glaciers. It's pretty simple, it shouldn't take you more than twenty minutes.'

If only reading was that simple! I thought.

Were reading that simple, I would have read every single book in my library at school. I would have read every encyclopedia that ever existed, and like a scuba diver I would have dived deep into the world of words, exploring them and maybe even making new words to describe the world around me.

'Don't worry, Mom, I will do it,' I said, trying to sound as casual as possible.

Mom was about to speak when Shlok interrupted her, 'Can Raghav and I go outside and play?'

'No. Raghav needs to complete his homework. Maybe he can play with you after he completes it, which I am doubtful of, considering how creative he can be in avoiding his homework.' Mom looked at me from the corner of her eye.

'But Mom,' Shlok pestered, 'yesterday Raghav had promised me he would help me to improve my running speed so that I could come first in the mini marathon race.'

'Not now, Shlok.' Mom's forehead creased into concerned wrinkles. 'I wish your brother would use some of that speed in his writing too. He runs like a cheetah but when it comes to reading and writing, he moves like a sloth!'

Sloth! I hated it when Mom talked about my reading speed like that. I didn't need anyone in the world to tell me I was a slow reader. I needed someone to help me read, if not fast, then at least like a normal kid.

'Please, Mom,' Shlok begged.

'No, Shlok, don't start with your "please" frenzy,' Mom said.

'Plllllleeeeeaaasssseee.' Shlok's 'please' had turned into a howl now! And when he did that Mom usually agreed but today she looked determined.

'NO, Shlok. Raghav has to complete his homework. I can't deal with anymore emails from his teacher complaining about him avoiding his homework, or informing me that his spelling grades are bad, or saying that he doesn't try hard enough to read. This year, he has to work harder!' Mom stated.

'Mom, Plleeeasssee,' Shlok pleaded again.

While Mom and Shlok continued their *NO,* and *Please* fight, no one thought to ask me what I wanted to do.

Of course, I'd rather go outside and play with Shlok, but if I didn't do my homework, Ms Joseph would make me stand outside the classroom.

And if I did do my homework, Ms Joseph would be in such a state of shock seeing my spellings that she would still make me stand out in the hallway.

I thought, and decided the best thing to do would be, not to do the homework because either way I would be standing out in the hallway during class.

'I am going to play with Shlok for some time, and I will work on my homework later,' I said, stuffing the sheet about melting glaciers in my bag. I was ready to escape the room.

'Yes, let's go!' Shlok yelled.

'But … Raghav … compl …' And before Mom said anything more, I sprinted out of our room, out of the house with Shlok right behind me.

We ran towards the park, my body slowly loosening up, and my legs picking up speed. After a claustrophobic day with Ms Joseph and her dreadful homework assignments, which was weighing down my mind, it felt like I was breathing freely for the first time.

The hot air heated my face, but even that felt cooler than the laughing and mocking of Karan. It was cooler than Ms Joseph's class, and definitely much cooler than Mom's shouting.

We joined the other boys in the park and quickly divided into teams. Shlok was always on my team.

We played till all of us were drained.

'We won! We WON!' Shlok yelled.

'Not fair, both of you always team up and win,' one of the boys complained.

'Yes! It's not fair. Next time, Raghav will be on my team,' the other boy said.

'No, he is my brother and best friend, and he will always be in my team,' Shlok shouted at them ready for a fight.

'Come on, Shlok, it's getting late, let's go home,' I said.

I thought it was funny that when I played sports, everyone wanted me on their team and, in the classroom, no one even wanted to sit next to me.

'You are the best, Raghav. You were so fast, that is why we won.' Shlok beamed at me with pride as we walked back home.

Shlok might be my younger brother but he always said the right words that made me feel good about myself and never judged me because of my writing or reading. That was one of the reasons I liked being with him.

'You are as fast as Usain Bolt,' he said. 'And one day, I am sure you are going to break his records.'

'That I will. But, before that, if I don't complete my homework, Mom will give me a medal for the boy who has broken his own records for not doing his work!' We both laughed as we entered the house.

But secretly, I knew better than Mom. It was I who wanted to do my work properly, it was I who yearned to read and write like a normal kid.

HOMEWORK HASSLES

Schoolwork that is a struggle

'Helll
oooo kids,' Papa jumped on us as soon as we entered the house.

Shlok leaped on his back and I ran into his outstretched arms. 'You are home early,' I said hugging him tightly.

'How was school?' he asked as he ruffled my hair.

Before I could open my mouth to tell him I had the worst day ever, Shlok leaped in and said, 'My day was SU—PERB, Papa! I love my new teacher. She is going to make us read lots of new books and she told me I was a very bright student because I answered all my spellings correctly!' Shlok jumped up and down with joy as he spoke.

'That's wonderful, and what about you, Sprinter?' he asked me.

After hearing about Shlok's perfect day. I didn't have the courage to tell Papa that even though I had decided this year I was going to do my best, I still couldn't make any sense of reading or writing and that made it a terrible day. So I lied, 'It was okay.'

'Raghav, your homework!' Mom yelled from the kitchen.

'Yes Mom,' I said softly, again feeling sick at the thought of working on two sheets.

'NOW, Raghav!' she screamed again from the kitchen.

'Come on, Sprinter, get down to work quickly then we will play everyone's favourite puzzle and quiz game,' Papa whispered and smiled.

My eyes widened with excitement. I loved playing with Papa. He always had something new and exciting for us to learn, and the best part? It didn't involve any reading or writing.

Mom came out of the kitchen with a spatula in her hand. 'Why are you still here, Raghav?' Her forehead creased in deep furrows.

'He was just going,' Papa said. 'Come on, champ.' He winked in my direction.

'Don't defend him, Shyam. He can't even write a single sentence without TEN spelling mistakes,' Mom said angrily.

'He is a smart boy, he will do it,' Papa pacified her.

Before Mom could say anything else, I went into my room thinking, I WILL DO IT! The thought of playing games with Papa excited me. I wanted to get done with my homework right away so that I could play with Papa.

I sharpened my pencil and looked at the sheet with fresh eyes. The glare of the letters hurt my eyes, and I squinted harder. It was a comprehension passage. So that meant you were supposed to read the passage and then answer the questions. That didn't sound very difficult.

I took out both the assignments from my bag and did a pinky-ponky of which one to start first. My finger landed on the global warming comprehension sheet. I decided to do that one first and leave the melting glaciers for later. I had seen a video on global warming and I was aware what a threat that was to the environment and if we didn't do something about it, the whole world would heat up like a big fireball sooner or later.

What could I do to reduce global warming? I was just ten years old. But Papa always says, 'If you want to change something, first begin the change with you.'

I began to daydream as I thought of a few solutions, maybe something simple to start with, like switching off the lights when I left the room. Or finding new sources of renewable energy like the sun. Mom used her computer a lot. If I could make solar cells that would save a lot of electricity.

I got more distracted and I thought of mobile phones, they emitted so much radiation. I wondered if I could create something to reduce the radiation, that would be wonderful! Maybe if I tried, I could partly solve this issue.

'Raghav! Are you doing your homework?' Mom called out from the living room.

I woke up from my invention dreams. Before I could invent anything to stop global warming, I had to find a way to read through this passage and answer the questions.

'Yes, Mom.'

I looked at the first line. The letters were standing in a straight row all waiting for the referee to say, 'Ready, Steady, Go!' And as soon as the whistle blew, off they went! They sprinted in all directions, because they didn't know where to go. They were lost, some ran to the right, some to the left and some kept spinning in spirals.

My pencil moved with my thoughts and I wrote exactly what I saw. I saw spinning spirals, so spirals were what I drew. Big spirals, small spirals, dark spirals, light spirals and I covered the entire sheet with lots and lots of spirals.

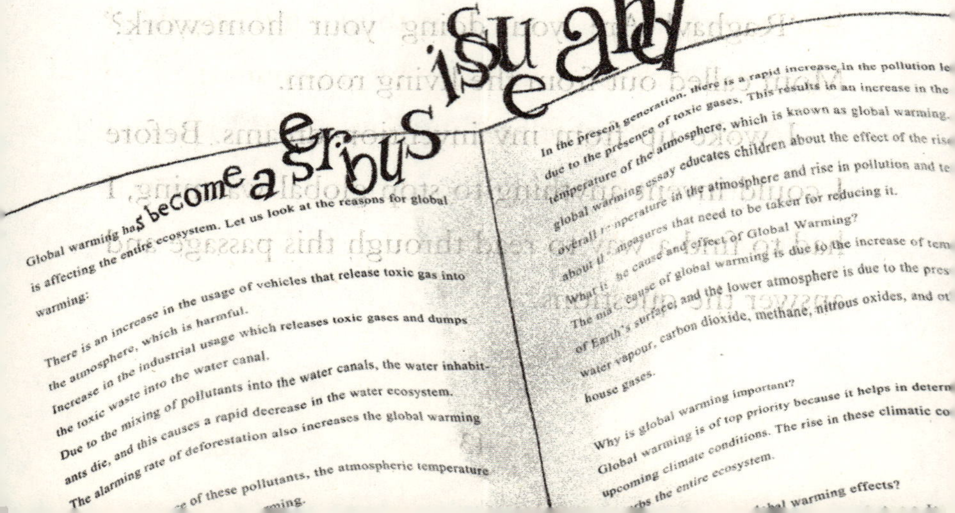

When my pencil stopped, lots of circles were on my paper. For a moment I was proud of the pattern I had created, I could see a combination of images bound together in a beautiful design!

Suddenly, I had a shooting pain in my tummy.

Ms Joseph did NOT give me a design assignment! She had given me a comprehension sheet!

I pressed my tummy hard hoping the pain would stop but it kicked back at me harder.

I decided to erase the circles, and in each part I erased, the paper tore a bit and left black marks. And soon I had tons of holes on my paper and lots of dirty black smudges. The beautiful pattern now looked like the messiest and dirtiest paper I had ever seen, and within seconds, without thinking, I shredded my homework sheet into tiny bits of confetti.

My eyes nearly fell off my face when I realized my brain was telling me to create a new pattern with the torn bits of paper!

'Raghav, are you done?' I heard Mom calling. And before she entered my room, I quickly threw all the bits of paper into the dustbin and took out the second sheet that I was supposed to do and placed it in front of me just in the nick of time.

She smiled on seeing me sitting at my desk. 'Good job,' she said.

My tummy howled with pain at the thought of what would happen if she peeped into the dustbin and saw the confetti.

She came closer. 'Oh Raghav! You haven't written a single word and it's already dinner time!' She sounded upset.

'M-my t-tummy is hurting,' I said holding my tummy real hard, and I was nearly in tears.

'Not another tummy ache, Raghav?' Mom asked.

I groaned. 'It's hurting a lot, Mom.' The truth was that it was hurting, but a little bit of acting to make it look worse would do no harm.

'I'll get you the pink liquid,' she said and went out, and instantly came back with a bottle and spoon.

I took the medicine. I did feel better and, because Mom didn't ask me to do my homework after that, I felt relieved. But I put on my sad and pained face throughout dinner and just nibbled on the food. I would rather starve than do my homework.

After dinner, we did some puzzles which I enjoyed very much and also played quiz games.

'Raghav, you've got every single question right today. Even the capitals that you had missed last time are all correct! You are superb at this!' Papa said with excitement.

'Awww! Raghav, you are the KING again! How do you always know these answers?' Shlok whined, disappointed that he had lost.

'I wish he'd use some of his brains in school too,' Mom said.

Mom was right. Why was I able to do everything really well except read and write? Wasn't that supposed to be the most important thing in the world? I quickly changed my happy face to the in-pain, sad-look face. I was excited about my win, but I didn't want Mom to think I felt better lest she remembered my homework.

'It's okay, he is good at other things,' Papa said.

'You are always supporting him and that is why he doesn't study hard,' Mom said.

Papa winked at me and said, 'You'd better buck up in school, kid, or else your Mom is not going to give you peace this year until you do better.'

I knew no one was going to give me peace, neither Mom, nor Ms Joseph, nor Karan. Finding solutions to global warming seemed so much easier.

That night under my aqua blue astronaut blanket, I dreamed I was hiding in a cave and a monster was hovering outside to eat me up. The monster looked like a hungry Ms Joseph who was waiting to eat up kids like me who didn't do their homework.

NERVOUS

Uneasiness about something with an uncertain outcome

Next morning, I begged Mom to let me stay at home. 'I am seriously ill and my tummy is going to explode and every single worm that I have in my stomach is going to fly around in your clean house,' I said, squeezing my tummy.

'Raghav, I would rather have the worms explode in school than in the house!' Mom said. 'Rush off now, but I am worried what your teacher is going to say about your incomplete homework. I wish you had done it.'

That was my worry too and that is why I wanted to stay at home but Mom would never agree. I tried my luck again. 'Should I stay back at home?' Her face stiffened and that was my warning to stop pushing her.

I'll tell Ms Joseph the truth, I thought. I'll tell her I wasn't feeling well. Though I knew Ms Joseph would never ever believe me.

On reaching school, my stomach started somersaulting again. I trudged my way to class and sat in my usual seat at the back of the classroom. I looked at Vedh from the corner of my eye. He was busy admiring Karan's new watch and Daksh kept saying, 'WOW! What a watch! It can even track the number of steps you walk in a day. Aren't you lucky and it's not even your birthday!'

I wondered how having a watch that counted steps was considered lucky. In my mind, the only people lucky were those who could read and write normally.

I wished I had an invisible potion. I'd drink it all even if it tasted terrible and then I would be invisible to Ms Joseph and her laser beam eyes. But I didn't have anything like that!

'Good morning class, I hope you all have done your homework? I'll come around and collect your sheets personally,' Ms Joseph said. Today Ms Joseph was dressed in a navy blue suit, which made her look like a military sergeant. I imagined her making us do drills of spelling and my head started spinning.

She started collecting the homework sheets without wasting any time. As she moved towards my desk, my legs began to shake, my heart stopped breathing. What would I tell her? Think, Raghav, think! Quick! My heart was going to come out of my skin and burst any moment.

What if I said my dog pooped on my homework? No! That was too lame. How about if I told her the rain washed my homework into the gutter? I glanced out the window at the clear blue sky! I tapped my feet harder, my face become numb, and still I couldn't come up with an excuse.

Maybe I could fool her with the old, I flushed my homework down the toilet excuse! No!

How about, my brother was pretending to be a dinosaur and he ate every single word! No!

What if I told her the truth? It was in a hundred pieces of tiny confetti at the bottom of my wastebasket at home!

I tried to imagine what I would say in my mind. 'Ms Joseph, I cannot tell a lie, I couldn't do my homework because the words moved across the paper like a Bollywood dancer with two left feet!' Now, that would be the truth—but there was no way I would tell her that in front of everybody. The last thing I wanted to do was admit that I couldn't read to the whole world.

I could foresee I was going to be in severe trouble and if she found out I had torn my homework into bits of paper, I would be standing in front of the principal's office.

Before I could think of anything else, Ms Joseph towered in front of me like a giant, and I felt like an ant that was about to be crushed. She said, 'Your homework, Raghav? Don't think I have forgotten, you had to submit two worksheets.'

'I–I . . .' My throat closed up and I couldn't speak. My mind flashed to one of the quiz questions Papa had asked, 'What is a person who can't speak called?' I had said, 'Aphasia.' With Ms Joseph standing at the firing line, I sure was experiencing what a person affected with aphasia felt. Complete mutism!

'Raghav, your homework!' She was getting impatient now and her eyes peeped into my brain with 1000x binocular vision and were searching my brain to see what excuses I had to tell her. I am sure she didn't see anything except a lot of entangled wires.

The whispering started.

'Same old story,' Karan whispered loud enough so that others could hear.

'He is so dumb!' Daksh followed.

'Karan and Daksh!' Ms Joseph said. 'If one more word escapes out of your mouth,' her eyes swept the room and landed on Karan, 'you will be standing outside the class for the rest of the day.'

'Raghav, where is the homework? Are you acting fresh with me?'

My face felt hot and my palms sweaty.

'I . . . I . . .' I froze and so did my words.

'There will be no recess for you today and during recess you will complete your work and hand it to me,' she said, her eyes still scanning my brain.

Wasn't she going to send me to the principal's office? She didn't even make me stand outside the class! Maybe our grade-four teacher had warned her that I was a waste of time. Or maybe when she had peeked into my brain with her binocular vision, she had seen my wires were miserably entangled and thought it was going to be useless to expect anything from me, so she just let me be!

Something like missing recess didn't seem like a punishment at all! Because I was used to staying inside since Vedh had joined Karan's gang. The truth was, I had no one to play with.

After explaining some maths concepts on the blackboard, Ms Joseph asked us to work on some maths sheets which I managed to complete just fine with the exception of a few word problems, which I skipped.

'Now we will do some popcorn reading,' Ms Joseph said.

'Yay!' Simran exclaimed.

I am in for another rotten day! I thought.

'What's popcorn reading?' Karan asked. 'Are we going to get cheese popcorn after we read?'

'That sounds yummy,' Vedh added.

Ms Joseph shot both of them a look and they both sat quietly.

'Popcorn reading is a game. I will randomly pick on anyone to read anytime. Especially, the ones who don't pay attention,' she locked her eyes with everyone, one by one as if she already knew who the useless kids were.

'So, take out your readers and we will read from page thirty-seven. And Karan, since you wanted some popcorn, you can start,' Ms Joseph said.

Karan quickly began to read. And I did my best not to get jealous, he made reading sound so easy.

I tried to look at my book as if I was really concentrating and was following what Karan was reading. There was no way I wanted to be picked on.

I turned the page when everyone else turned theirs and that's when I got the brilliant idea to use my finger to tap on each word as I heard it being spoken! At last, I was confident I would at least know where everyone was in the book!

I continued to tap each word as Ms Joseph asked Vedh to read. But then the quiet girl, Neetu, was called on. She read so softly I could hardly hear her. And that is when I lost my place on the page.

When it was Simran's turn to read, she read flawlessly. She was so good; she made different funny voices for each of the characters! I got so excited by the story, I started to watch her face as she read and I forgot what I was supposed to be doing, which was following along in the book.

I wished she would continue to read but suddenly I heard, 'RAGHAV.'

I wasn't even aware which paragraph we were on! I quickly looked at the watch.

There was ten full minutes left for recess. I stood up confidently but my insides felt like a tub of mushy, runny ice cream.

Karan covered his mouth and laughed. Daksh copied him. I was sure Daksh would follow him straight into a well, if Karan declared well diving the latest and greatest sport.

By now Karan and his gang's laughing and teasing shouldn't have been bothering me. After all, it was like an everyday routine like brushing, eating and breathing. But from the time Vedh had joined them, I was sick from inside.

The word sick has two meanings, one where you feel physically sick because of an illness, and the second when you felt sick because someone made you feel fed up about yourself. I felt the second type of sick.

'Raghav, will you start reading,' Ms Joseph's voice thundered.

'Y-yes ...' I stammered.

I started to read, and immediately everyone in class broke out laughing.

'We've already read that,' Karan said, rolling his eyes.

'He doesn't even know where we are,' Daksh said.

'Silence, Karan and Daksh, I think I am the teacher here and not the two of you!' Ms Joseph said.

'Raghav, why aren't you concentrating?' Ms Joseph asked, frowning.

'It's the paragraph after that one,' Simran whispered so that no one could hear her.

I started again. And I was so slow. I spoke each word carefully, sounding out different sounds until I got it right. Or, at least I hoped I got it right! My face flushed, my reading was precisely like Mom had said, like a sloth.

I heard long sighs and the sound of heads falling on tables as if my reading was making everyone sleepy. Simran helped me with a few words and I was relieved to find I had finished reading the first line. The recess bell rang! Talk about being saved by the bell.

'I am glad we are saved from the torture of hearing Raghav read,' Karan said.

Vedh said, 'He can't read for nuts!'

I acted as if I couldn't hear Vedh because sometimes it's good to be deaf to a lot of things. Not hearing other people's opinions saves you from the trouble of feeling low and thinking little of yourself.

DREAMS FADING AWAY

A cherished ambition

Gradually grow faint and disappear

During recess Simran, the girl in the wheelchair, and I were the only two left in class.

'Thanks for helping me read,' I said softly.

She smiled. Even though none of the girls were talking to her or had tried to befriend her, she was always beaming and happy in her own world. I wondered how she managed that.

'Why don't you go out for recess?' I asked.

'It's difficult to maneuver my chair with too many people around and they might just knock me down,' she said, as she opened her lunch box and took a bite of her puri aloo.

Hmmm … Yummy, I thought!

I quickly gobbled my cheese and tomato sandwich which, I was certain, tasted poor compared to Simran's mouth-watering lunch.

'Why didn't you do your homework? And why do these boys bully you?' Simran asked.

No one had ever asked me that question before, because by now everyone thought of me as the class dummy. And everyone knows that dummies are always the ones who get teased and pushed around.

If I admitted to Simran that I had done my homework except that I had drawn spirals on it though I meant to make words and letters even she would think I was wooden headed. So, I just shrugged my shoulders trying to act cool on the outside, even if I didn't feel that way inside!

And I quietly avoided her second question on bullying, because that didn't need any explanation! She would soon find out on her own anyway.

Instead, I offered her a cookie.

'Yummy. You'd better start working on your assignment or Ms Joseph will get angry with you,' she said as she sputtered crumbs.

'Yes, you are right.' I carefully centered the homework sheet Ms Joseph had given me on my desk.

Simran buried herself in her book. I longed to read as easily she could. I wanted nothing more than to bury myself in an exciting story as the world around me disappeared.

As I looked at my homework sheet, nothing made sense. I remembered Mom told me the assignment was about melting glaciers and I felt confident of that part. I had already learned a lot about glaciers from the videos Shlok and I watched with Papa.

I took a deep breath and wrote, 'Galcirs ra weri emprtnt for the inviramant as they tell us abut zanging tamprechurs. Glaciars are the larjest sorse of frash vater in the warld. If the Entartic sheet malted the se leval wuld rize.' I was relieved that I finally wrote something down.

I suddenly wanted to write more and fill the entire sheet. I had so much to share about glaciers! I remembered that if temperatures kept rising, the glaciers would melt very fast. And in the last fifty years, a lot of the world's ice had melted because of global warming and if the ice continued to melt like this, the sea level would rise. And scientists were worried that whole cities could go under water.

I was still imagining which cities would go under water when the bell rang and recess was over.

I heard a loud rapping on my desk!

'Have you done your work?' Karan asked, standing in front my desk.

'Why should I tell you?' I said trying to be confident.

The next thing I knew Karan swiped his arm on my desk. Everything dropped to the floor. My pens, pencils, eraser, ruler and my elephant key chain—all lying on the floor. Even the glacier homework sheet which I had just worked on! My face started to warm up and my eyes filled with stingy tears.

Karan picked up my homework sheet with two fingers as if it was nothing but a dirty piece of cloth. 'Daksh, Vedh, come over and check out Raghav's homework sheet!' He said and he burst out laughing.

Not again! I thought.

'What's a gal-cir?' he asked everyone who had crowded around my desk as if he was a quizmaster.

'I've never heard of anything like that,' Daksh said confused.

Karan passed my homework paper to Vedh.

I bit my lip.

'I think the word is glacier,' Vedh said, avoiding my eyes.

'What! That's glacier? Who would write such a spelling for glaciers?' Karan laughed as if that was the funniest joke he had ever cracked.

'How dumb!' one of the boys said.

'He is such a weirdo!' another one said.

'Pass my paper back,' I said, my jaw tightening up.

Karan ignored what I said; instead, he made an airplane out of my paper and released it into the air. I lunged for the airplane before it flew in circles, but I missed. Just as Ms Joseph entered class, it made a three-point landing on her desk.

I froze.

Karan and the others quickly took their seats as if they had done nothing wrong.

Ms Joseph unfolded the paper and her eyes scanned through my carefully scrawled words. I nervously watched her forehead crease. She squinted at the paper with dangerously close attention.

My shoulders tensed up.

'Is this your assignment, Raghav?' she asked.

I nodded, looking at my shoes which were not polished.

'Go back to your seat, and I will not tolerate any child to be bullied in my class. I hope I have made that clear to all of you!' Ms Joseph said, and then she kept looking at my paper as if she had never seen anything like this before.

GEOGRAP
GEOG

My mind flashed back in time to the rock museum I had visited during the holidays. The museum had a red stone that I couldn't help staring at. But my homework was not beautiful like the stone. My homework was a tangled mess of ugly spellings! There was nothing worth looking at on the paper.

I wondered if Ms Joseph was going to keep my homework in a frame above her desk and display it to all the students in the coming years. I would become a school legend and she would tell all of them, 'This was the boy who just couldn't write and I don't want any of you to be like him!'

'Why didn't you tell Ms Joseph about Karan?' Simran whispered as soon as I sat on my seat.

But what could I tell her? That Karan and his friends make fun of me. They push me around and that my best friend has left me because he wants to be with the important boys and that however hard I try, I can't read and write.

'What about the second sheet, Raghav?' Ms Joseph asked. 'You have handed me only one.'

'I-I couldn't do it,' I blurted out.

'He never does his homework,' Karan said.

'Yes, Ms Joseph, even last year Mr Gupta gave up on him,' Daksh said. I wondered if Daksh would ever use his own mind and express his own opinion. I think he had locked his brains up and kept it safely somewhere, where even he wouldn't find them!

'I haven't asked for your opinion on Raghav's homework, Karan and Daksh, and I believe Raghav has a mouth to speak for himself.' She shot one of her guns at them.

'Raghav, this is your last warning.' She narrowed her eyes at me and I knew she meant it.

I nodded, already feeling nervous about the next assignment she was going to give me.

Ms Joseph moved on to geography. We learnt

about latitudes and longitudes. I enjoyed the class, as we didn't have to write anything.

'Can anyone tell me, if we were staying in India, would London be ahead of us in time or behind?' Ms Joseph asked.

I quickly shot my hand up.

'Yes, Raghav,' she said.

'Behind, Ms Joseph,' I said.

'Good,' she said.

Karan murmured something to Vedh and they both silently laughed. I might not be good at noticing my own spelling mistakes, but I had become pretty good at noticing others laugh at me even when they used their silent laugh, and it poked like a nail in the head, in the stomach and everywhere where else I could imagine.

Ms Joseph asked us a few more questions and I raised my hand for all of them, and she let me answer most of them.

'I am giving out a list of words and we will have a spelling test tomorrow,' Ms Joseph said.

A spelling test! Wow! I thought, another reason for me to be mocked.

I sat up all evening attempting to learn the words Ms Joseph had given. I didn't even play with Papa or Shlok. I put the spellings in my brain and let them sit there, the rounded O's, the flat F, and the curvy S, and at one moment, I felt 100 per cent confident that I knew the spellings, and in another, I was lost in space with the letters turning into spaceships darting everywhere around the planet Earth.

Next day, after the spelling test, Ms Joseph collected our sheets. She examined mine and moved on.

I was dizzy when I looked at Simran's sheet after Ms Joseph gave them back to us. She had scored a 10/10! I tried to hide my marks but Simran still saw them. In spite of my best efforts, I still scored a zero.

By now I was sure she thought I was the stupidest person in the universe. Sometimes, I wondered if everyone was right! And I did deserve to be bullied!

For the next two weeks, I worked hard to do all the sheets Ms Joseph gave me. I knew they were not even worth looking at because my handwriting looked like they were worms crawling. Sometimes it was difficult for me to read what I had written. So, I didn't expect others to understand what I had written.

Ms Joseph completely stopped trying with me. She did not say a word to me about my work. Ms Joseph told me she had twenty years of experience working as a teacher and no student had fooled her yet! She was right! I hadn't fooled her. She was a good teacher. She

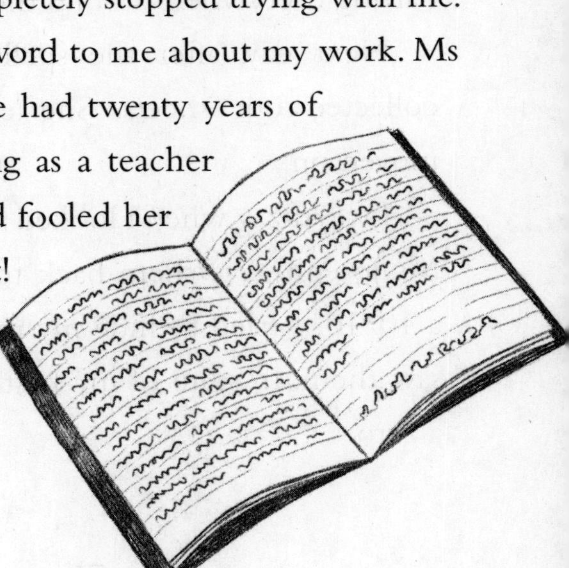

had simply given up on me! I was certain she had decided that I was one of those kids she didn't want to waste her time on.

As I thought about that, tears began to emerge and I knew this year was going to be one of the worst years as the teacher had backed off from me already, and my dream of learning to read and write faded.

TEARS SPILL

Salty liquid that comes out of a person's eye when they cry

Liquid falling over the edge unintentionally

'Raghav,' Ms Joseph called out as soon as I stood up with my bag to leave for home.

For a moment I debated with myself if I had really heard my name. I turned around and discovered her looking at me. I took tiny steps towards her desk, asking myself what would a teacher want from me?

Ms Joseph handed me a white envelope and said, 'Please give this to your parents and tell them I want to meet them tomorrow.'

'Sure,' I said casually, but my brain cells immediately started a crazy roller-coaster ride of WHYs! Why did she want to meet Mom and Papa? Did she get sick of me, and now wants to throw me out of her class? Was she going to tell Mom and Papa that her class only had bright students and not dumb ones like me? Did she plan to tell them to keep me home!

My hands itched to open the envelope but it was sealed with tape and was addressed to Papa and Mom. I waited for Papa to come home. I didn't want to give the envelope to Mom. If the atom bomb was getting ready to explode, it better be in front of Papa. At least, there would be a chance of survival.

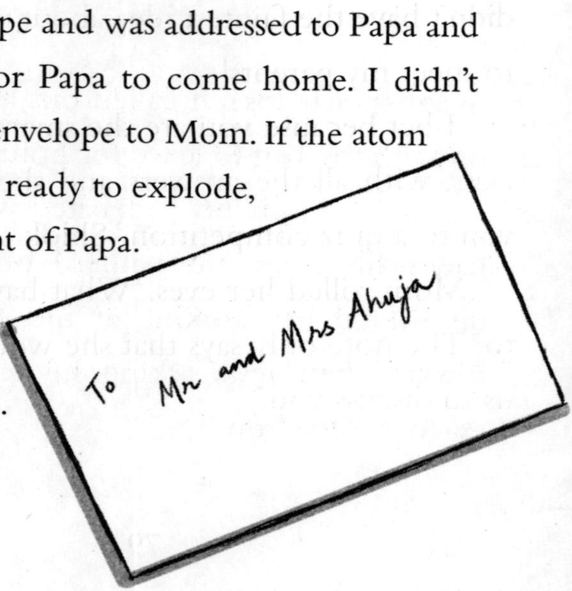

'Papa, my teacher gave this envelope and told me to give it to you.' Mom's eyes widened. 'And … she said she wanted to meet you b-both tomorrow,' I stammered.

Papa tore the seal and read the note. He handed it over to Mom.

'Why does your teacher want to meet Mom and Papa?' Shlok asked.

I hushed him.

Mom read the note and said, 'What is this, Raghav? Why does she want to meet us?'

'I wish I knew,' I said. I was speaking the truth. I didn't have the faintest idea about why she wanted to meet my parents!

'I bet because you are the smartest boy in your class, with all the answers and she wants to send you to a quiz competition,' Shlok said.

Mom rolled her eyes. 'What have you been up to? The note only says that she would like to meet us to discuss you.'

I shrugged my shoulders. What was there to discuss about me? I thought.

'Let's not make up stories about what it might be. Let's just go and meet her tomorrow,' Papa suggested.

'Yes,' Mom said, but worry took over her face.

'Now, now, there's nothing to worry. Raghav is a smart kid,' Papa said.

'Sometimes I think you're the only one who thinks that. None of his teachers have ever said he is a smart kid. They've always complained that he shirks work and is a lazy boy. He will write one spelling correct and then he will misspell the same one again later!' Mom put her hand on her forehead.

It was true. Every teacher was fed up of me and none of them wanted me in their class. Even though I had never been the troublemaker, I was still the kid who knew nothing!

'It's going to be okay,' Papa said.

I wondered how? And I thought Mom's worried face was asking the same question. HOW?

Next day, Papa, Mom and I were sitting with Ms Joseph in a small grey room. My heart was beating like a drum. I kept checking Papa's face to see whether he could hear the drumming!

A small table neatly stacked with papers stood in between Ms Joseph and us. Wooden shelves of thick, thin, big and small books covered her walls and since the walls weren't big enough to hold all her books, big piles of books were stacked on the floor. There was barely enough room to squeeze into the room. I worried if Papa were to attempt to get a little comfortable, he would be sure to topple some of the books. I couldn't imagine anyone having so many books unless they were a library! Did she read so many books?

And then a sudden thought started to sting me like a bee, which hurt—would I be able to read a single one of these books?

Before Ms Joseph began, Mom spilled out her worries. Papa had warned her not to talk before the teacher spoke but she couldn't control herself. 'I know Raghav has not been a good student. He messes up with his spellings a lot but he does work hard. I don't know why he can't be like my younger son, who is excellent in his studies,' Mom said.

Ms Joseph looked at Mom with calm soft eyes I had never seen her use before. They were so different from the dagger eyes she used in class. She said, 'He is a different child. His brain is wired differently than your younger son.'

See! I always knew that she could see my brain with her binocular vision. Mom looked puzzled but quickly said, 'I have decided to get him a tutor who will help him with his reading and writing.'

DICTIONARY
ENCYCLOPAEDIA
ATLAS
BOOKOFINDIAN POETS
GANDHI
AMBEDKAR
FUN

'Your son is a very bright student,' Ms Joseph said.

I nearly fell off my chair. Bright! Me?

'I always told you our boy is smart!' Papa said.

Mom looked more puzzled than ever before.

'Yes, Raghav is a smart boy with a lot of knowledge about many different things,' Ms Joseph said.

Yes! I did have a lot of knowledge about a lot of things! Like how it feels when you are lonely! How it feels when you are called dumb! And how it feels when your best friend leaves you for a boy who is a bully!

Papa looked impressed but Mom seemed to be in an unbelievable world, one where I was a bright student! I understood why she was having a hard time, because I was struggling a little bit with this new idea myself!

'We need to help Raghav to use his smartness in his reading and writing as well,' Ms Joseph said.

Mom's eyes switched from me to Papa, and then to Ms Joseph.

'What do you mean?' Mom asked.

'I cannot say this definitely without the specialist giving Raghav a few tests, but in addition to his being bright and smart, he has a difficulty in reading and writing,' Ms Joseph said.

'Specialist? Tests? What's this all about? Why would my son need a specialist?' Mom was starting to lose her mind now.

Papa squeezed her hand.

'Please don't worry,' Ms Joseph said kindly. 'These tests are simple and they will help the specialist understand his difficulty level and, with a little help, he will soon be at par with the other kids,' Ms Joseph said.

AT PAR WITH OTHER KIDS! I repeated in my mind. That's what I always wanted to be. That meant I would read and write like them!

'Why him? What's wrong with him?' Mom asked.

'There is nothing wrong with him. Does Raghav struggle with his homework?' Ms Joseph asked.

Mom nodded. I nodded too.

'Does he try hard and still seem unable to do his school work,' Ms Joseph asked again.

'Always,' Mom said.

I nodded.

'Does he get confused between letters?' she asked.

Mom and I both nodded our heads.

'Raghav understands complex things easily in class. They are things which other students have difficulty in understanding. He always raises his hand to answer but when the same question is put on paper, he can't do it.' Ms Joseph spoke as if she had known me forever and the best part was that she was saying all this without making a stinking deal about it.

It's like when you say someone is having a problem, but do it kindly with your best intention to help them. It was so different from being told the other way when you announce bad news to someone with the intention to hurt them. Ms Joseph was the very first person to tell me about my problem with kindness.

I kept nodding *yes* like a bobble head to everything she said.

'I cannot say for sure but I truly think Raghav will be able to perform better if he is given the right direction,' Ms Joseph said reassuringly, which warmed my heart.

I felt my eyes prick and I let the tears spill. I always wanted to hide my weakness because I was afraid of people judging me and making fun of me. But Ms Joseph had seen right through my skin and wanted to help me! I had been wrong about her. She did see me. And now she wanted to help me become a NORMAL kid, and that is what I wanted more than anything in the world!

'But ... my son is fine,' Mom pressed again.

'NO ...' I hated to admit it but I had to say it someday, 'I am not fine.' Usually in such times my voice runs to a safe place to hide out. But today I surprised myself as I blurted out something I had never admitted to anyone before, not even to myself. All three of them stared at me, and I could feel the hair on my head stand up.

'I think Raghav is right. We will go through with these tests,' Papa said.

Mom was quiet. I couldn't tell what she was thinking.

'So, Raghav, I will set up a time with the school specialist and you can see her tomorrow,' Ms Joseph said.

'But will I be able to do these tests?' I whispered.

'Of course, they are especially designed so you can answer the questions with ease,' said Ms Joseph and smiled.

It was the first time I saw Ms Joseph smile and I had made the huge mistake of thinking she was Hitler. I had been wrong about that, too. I was slowly beginning to discover that Ms Joseph was not a bad teacher. She wasn't even a normal teacher. She was a GREAT teacher.

'Are you okay with this?' Papa asked me on our way back.

If there was anything I was okay with—it was meeting the specialist if she could help me to read and write.

I played with Shlok all evening. We raced each other and I taught him some tricks on improving his speed. 'You must be the fastest runner in your class?' Shlok looked at me enviously.

'Yes, every year I win all the golds.' And that is why Karan hates me because he wins all the silvers, I thought.

'And did your teacher tell Mom and Papa that you are the brightest kid in her class and that you know everything in the whole wide world there is to know? Maybe you should enter a contest of the BOY WHO KNOWS EVERYTHING!' His eyes widened with excitement.

I smiled at his innocence. Shlok was not aware that what came easily to him was one of my biggest weaknesses. I had a lot of learning ahead of me, and the truth was, I was excited! I had finally found my opportunity to begin learning from scratch.

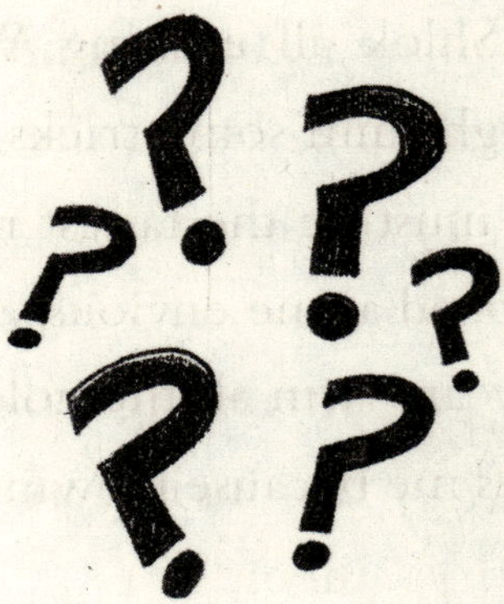

CHOICES

An act of choosing between two or more possibilities

I crossed my fingers before entering the resource room where I would meet the specialist.

'Hi, you must be Raghav?' A woman, with short curly hair and much younger looking than Ms Joseph, asked me. She had a box full of paints in her hands.

'Yes,' I said.

'You are right on time. I am Isha, please take a seat,' she said, as she set a paint box full of bright colours in a corner. I noticed lots of interesting looking things that invited me to play with them.

'So, Raghav, you are here to take some tests, but these are not the usual kind. I guarantee that these tests are a lot of fun!' She smiled.

I took the test. And Ms Isha hadn't lied! It wasn't a usual school test. Instead, it was fun and interesting. Well, most of it, except a few parts, which I couldn't do. It seemed like a very, very long time before Ms Isha said, 'I think we are done, Raghav.'

As I put my pencil in my book bag, Ms Isha looked right into my eyes and said, 'Raghav, whatever the results of this test might be, I want you to know that we all have some difficulties in our lives. And I also want you to understand that I am here to support you. I hope, as time goes by, you will recognize me as a friend.'

I don't know why but I believed every word Ms Isha said, and I decided that Ms Isha seemed like a nice teacher.

I reached class late, but Ms Joseph let me in without saying a word.

'How come Raghav is allowed in class even if he is late?' Karan opened his big mouth and made my absence visible to those who hadn't even noticed that I was not in my usual place at the back of the room!

Ms Joseph's face hardened as she opened her mouth to speak to Karan, when the class loudspeaker crackled on.

'Hello fifth graders!' a loud, energetic voice came out from the speaker. I instantly guessed it was Mr Bolt, our athletics teacher! And I bet he had something special to say!

'We are beginning athletics practice after school, starting today. All of those students who want to take part in the athletics competition, please give your names to your teachers so that they can send an email to your parents about your staying after school to practise,' he announced.

'Wow!' I thought! This was the day I waited for every year!

The speaker crackled to life again. 'Even those who have never thought to try out before, this is a good day to join us to see what you can do. And don't forget!

Leave all your worries behind and bring your "A" game to the field.'

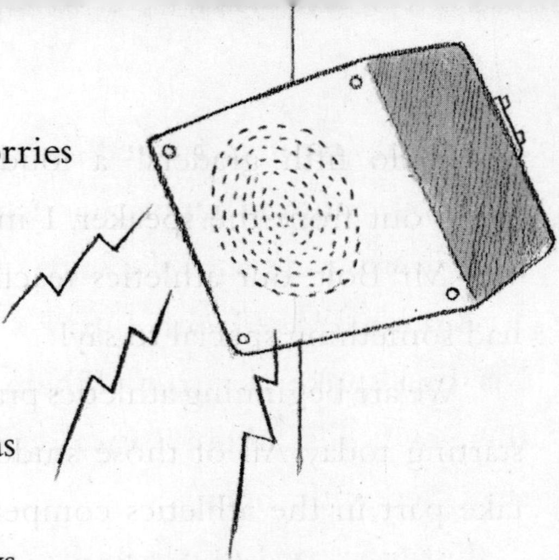

Mr Bolt's voice was as energetic as his drills.

Mr Bolt always encouraged everyone to run but I didn't need any encouragement, I just needed an empty track expanding before me and I would run, run and run! Because I loved running!

I was first in line to give my name to Ms Joseph. Karan, Vedh, Daksh and a few other girls and boys were behind me.

My body was buzzing all over with excitement but when I looked at Simran, her head hung down and she seemed unusually tiny on her wheelchair. I even noticed that her lower lip stuck out a kilometre.

‘What’s wrong?’ I asked her.

‘I love running but because I am in a wheelchair, I obviously can’t run,’ she said.

Simran looked sad. I had a sudden thought. Ms Isha spoke the truth. There are people with their own difficulties. I was not the only one who struggled with them.

Just like that I understood Simran and the pain she felt. I wondered how I could support her and let her know I cared.

‘You want a cookie?’ I asked, trying to cheer her up.

‘No,’ she said, still looking grumpy.

‘But the wheelchair is not going to be with you forever,’ I said.

She suddenly broke into a smile. ‘Yes, you are right! I can run next year!’ Then she asked, ‘Can I still have the cookie, Raghav?’

‘Sure,’ I said, happy that she was not sulking anymore.

Later in the field, I geared myself up for the run. I did some jumps, knee raises and a few laps of track, which Mr Bolt was very particular about. He always said, 'Warm-ups are very important.'

Soon Mr Bolt whistled, and we all gathered around him. He spoke in a scream-yell kind of voice so that everyone could hear him. 'Today, I am going to write down your timings for all the events and then every day we are going to practise after school so that you all can improve your timings.'

My legs already felt the itch to run. I started jumping in my place, just like boxers do.

'Raghav, I see you are already excited to run, but this time it's going to be tough competition,' Mr Bolt said.

I jumped higher and did a few more knee raises.

'After two weeks, I am going to retake your timings and the kids with the best timings will take part in the race three weeks from now!' He hollered as if we were two football fields away, and we couldn't hear him.

The whistle went off again and we took our positions. Vedh stood right next to me. For a happy moment, it felt like old times, when he would say, 'Come on, Sprinter, do it.' But he didn't say anything this time.

Mr Bolt screamed, 'Ready, steady, GO!'

I took the leap. My legs did their work as my mind focused on the finish line. I pushed harder and kept telling myself to go faster! Faster! I could feel Karan right next to me. If I didn't push harder, he would pass me anytime. I pushed with everything I had in me and reached the finish line with Karan nearly stepping on my heels!

I gave out a big sigh of relief. Phew! I beat him in just a few milliseconds. I would have to practise harder this year. Somehow, Karan's speed had increased from last year. I worried I had a battle ahead of me, and it was not going to be easy, just as Mr Bolt had said.

'That was a good run, Raghav, but Karan is not far behind you. You will need to maintain high speed throughout the run, and increase your stamina,' Mr Bolt said.

'You ran well,' Daksh told Karan.

'Yeah! But next time, I will be better prepared,' said Karan as he looked at me from the corner of his eye. He seemed to be warning me, 'WATCH OUT, I AM COMING.'

After a few more runs, we packed up for the day.

I made a mind map of practising every day after school with Mr Bolt to increase my speed. There was no way I was going to miss out on this opportunity to practise my running. Nothing was going to stand in the way of my winning the gold again this year!

I went for a few more tests with Ms Isha and then she called Mom after a few days, and confirmed that I did have learning difficulties. In other words, she said, I struggle with dyslexia.

'So, am I dumb?' I instantly asked.

'Of course not,' Papa said. He pulled me towards him, looked into my eyes and said, 'Dyslexia is not anywhere close to being dumb. It is only a disorder in interpreting words, which can be dealt with.'

I still felt weird and different, just like Simran must feel as she sits in her wheelchair. My challenges were now visible for everyone to see.

'Can this big X-word disease be cured?' Shlok asked, looking anxious.

'Shlok, I want you to understand that Raghav doesn't have a disease! Raghav has a superb brain! It's just that when it comes to reading and writing, there are a few rocks in the way on which he stumbles. The specialist teacher is going to help him remove those rocks.' Papa reached for his laptop and typed into the search bar and showed us a picture.

I recognized the first picture and said,

'Muhammad Ali, the boxing champ!'

'He struggled with dyslexia,' Papa said.

My eyes became really big! Muhammad Ali struggled with dyslexia that means his brain was wired similar to mine!

Next, he showed me a picture of someone I didn't recognize.

'That's Tom Cruise,' Papa said.

'The guy who made all those cool action-packed movies?' Shlok asked.

'Yes. He was challenged with dyslexia too,' Papa told us.

'Wow!' Shlok said. 'So does being dyslexic mean you have an awesome brain?'

'Yes! It means you are good at a lot of things that are difficult for others to do easily,' Papa said.

Papa described my brain as if it was something exceptional. He showed us lots of pictures of artists, comedians, actors and writers who were challenged by dyslexia.

'Wow! I didn't know Raghav has a special brain! The big X thing is not a disease! And he is going to be famous one day! How lucky you are!' Shlok said with his admiring eyes looking right at me.

I was so happy to know that I was not dumb in the way Karan and the others thought. I now knew I had a problem that other smart people had overcome. It had a name, and with it, I understood myself better. Dyslexia! I was not the only one in the whole world who felt that way. And for the first time I felt confident that I could overcome it with my ability to remember things quickly and with Ms Isha's help.

'What's the teacher's plan for him?' Papa asked.

'She wants to meet him three days a week after school, and two days a week in between classes,' Mom said.

'AFTER SCHOOL?' I asked.

Ms Isha wanted to meet me after school to help me and Mr Bolt wanted to meet me after school for my running practice!

Now what! I was STUCK!

Both running and learning to read and write were important to me. Why did they have to happen together? All this while, no one was helping me and suddenly everyone wanted to help me at the same time.

'Is there a problem, Raghav? We can wait before we start with Ms Isha,' Papa said, seeing my troubled face.

'Yes, I want you to be sure of what it is you want to do,' said Mom.

Winning the gold medals was very important to me! But learning to read and write was something I had been longing to do for forever.

Every time I heard Simran read out loud, it pained me to be reminded about what I couldn't do. And when other kids did their homework well,

I always felt a pinch in my conscience about not doing my work properly.

Running was important to me. My dream of breaking all the records of every single runner in the world was strong! BUT right now, learning to read and write were two things that I decided I wanted the most! And I was not going to miss this chance even if that meant only two days a week to practise with Mr Bolt.

'I've made up my mind. I am ready to work with Ms Isha,' I said. 'But, is it okay if I practise running the other two days when I am not with Ms Isha?' I asked.

'Sure, why not, and I will confirm with Ms Isha about you meeting her,' Mom said.

I would give up anything in the world to read and write, even if it meant giving up something I loved to do and that was running!

FRIENDS

A person with whom one has a bond and who accepts you the way you are

Classes with Ms Isha were fun but a lot of work. She made everything interesting and had many exciting ways to help me learn the simplest things. And this made me happy because it had been the simplest things that were difficult for me.

I had never slogged so hard but I liked every moment of it. I didn't miss a single class though my legs itched to run on the field. I knew I might lose the race on the final day, which was very close, but working with Ms Isha was more important to me.

Ms Isha did various activities with me, which she said would help me read and write. The one I liked the best was the sound game where she taught me sounds of different letters with the help of flash cards. Also, by using different materials like foam, sand and paint, learning seemed very fascinating. She even played lots of games with me. She beat me in two games and then I managed to beat her in one!

'Awesome, Raghav, you've learned things very quickly,' Ms Isha said.

Her words boosted my confidence!

Some days, she just talked to me, 'What are your hobbies, Raghav?'

'I love running. I love playing all kinds of games, especially the ones I play with my Papa and Shlok and ...' I paused and said, 'I like listening to Simran read and I want to read as well as she does one day.'

Ms Isha had this weird nice way of looking, and I knew she was going to say something to make me feel good. She said, 'Of course you are going to soon start to read, and maybe even better than Simran.'

I even told her about what I don't like: Karan's nagging at me, Daksh blindly following Karan's every order, and my disappointment at the way Vedh joined Karan's gang.

Ms Isha had her own thoughts on this. 'People can be mean and unreasonable,' she said with a wink, 'so it doesn't matter what they say. And if your former best friend has made friends with someone else that means he never was your type of best friend. You will surely find someone who is truly your friend and will accept you the way you are.' Ms Isha squeezed my hand with a smile, and somehow her words comforted me.

I agreed with Ms Isha's thoughts as I mulled over what she had said. Why was I so stuck with the idea of Vedh being my friend anyway?

During the regular school classes with Ms Joseph, things were easier now. She didn't ask me to read aloud. She didn't give me any written homework and didn't force me to write in class. She also excused me from the reading list she had put up and the book review reports.

'How come Ms Joseph doesn't give you any homework? I better remind her that she misses you each time she distributes the homework,' Karan started off again.

I wondered if all Karan did was watch my every move and judge me!

'Ms Joseph, you haven't been giving Raghav any written work. You give us extra sheets for homework, but you don't give him a single sheet. That's not fair!' Karan complained to Ms Joseph.

Ms Joseph gave Karan the kind of look that teachers gave to students who thought they were one step ahead of the teacher. I was certain she was going to give him a piece of her mind today!

'Well, Karan, have you heard of the word "difficulty"?' she asked him with daggers in her eyes.

Was she going to talk about my difficulty in front of the whole class? Was everybody going to know that I have issues with reading and writing?

But just then another thought crossed my mind, why should I hide it? Everybody knew Muhammad Ali's brain was special. So, if I had a special brain, what did I have to be scared about? Why didn't I want anyone to know about it? And Papa, Mom and Ms Isha had said that I was special.

'Yes, Ms Joseph, difficulty means it is harder to do normal things,' Karan said.

'Is there something that is difficult for you to do?' She didn't move her gaze from him.

'No. I can do everything,' he said softly, and shrank in his chair. Ms Joseph's eyes penetrated deeper and Karan shook like a cornered mouse.

'Well, you should be thankful to God that you find things easy!' Ms Joseph said sharply. 'But there are lots of people in the world who struggle with a lot of different things! With a little help, they are able to learn new ways to do them!'

Everyone was quiet, super quiet.

'Raghav is a very smart student. It is true he has some difficulties in reading and writing, and with help from Ms Isha, he will overcome these difficulties,' Ms Joseph said it so easily as if difficulties were normal.

Karan shifted in his chair.

I wondered what everybody was thinking.

Simran raised her hand.

'Since I had my accident, I am going to be in my wheelchair for some time, but with therapy I will be able to get over my difficulty.' Simran looked at me and smiled. A smile that you give to people when you want them to be comfortable.

Neetu, the shy girl, raised her hand.

'Yes, Neetu.'

'I have a difficulty too. I am shy.' She spoke very softly, then waited for a few seconds and said, 'But I have joined d-dancing c-classes to help me overcome my shyness.'

Another boy raised his hand and said, 'I have a difficulty too. I wear braces on my teeth. But when I complain, my mother says that I am lucky to wear them at this age so that when I turn older, I won't need them anymore, and I will have nice straight teeth.'

Ms Joseph nodded to everything everyone said. I saw her break into a soft smile. She said, 'I am proud of this batch of students who understand the meaning of "difficulties" so well.' She looked at Karan, who seemed to be sliding in his seat so low that no one could see him.

During recess, I decided not to go out. Instead, I took out a sheet of paper and wrote.

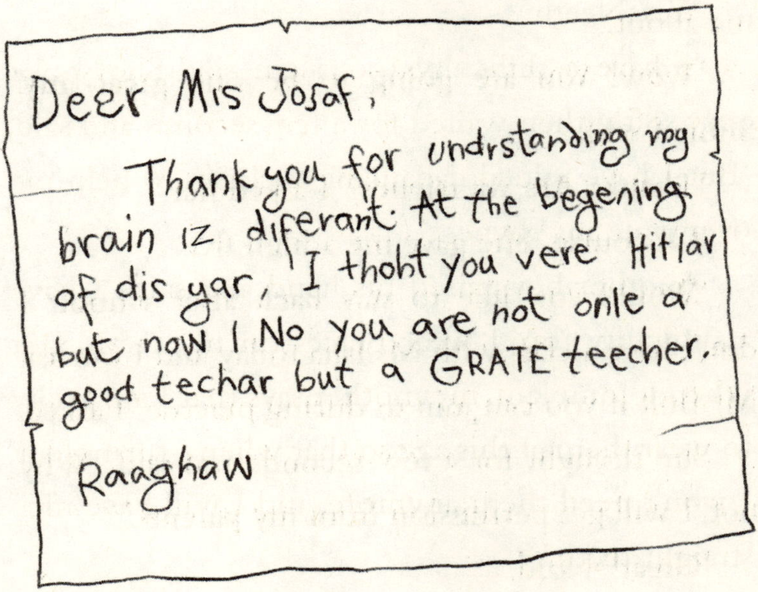

Deer Mis Josaf,

Thank you for undrstanding my
brain iz diferant. At the begening
of dis yar, I thoht you vere Hitlar
but now I No you are not onle a
good techar but a GRATE teecher.

Raaghaw

I hesitated about calling her Hitler, but finally decided to keep it and put the note on Ms Joseph's desk later.

'Hey Raghav,' Simran said, rolling her wheelchair towards me, 'I am sorry about the difficulty thing.'

'That's okay, you don't need to be sorry about it, my brain is just wired differently.' And then I told her about all the famous people Papa had told me about.

'Wow! You are going to be one great guy,' Simran said.

'Thanks. Are we friends?' I asked her.

'Of course.' She gave me a high five.

'Would you like to stay back after school? I don't have a class with Ms Isha today and I can ask Mr Bolt if you can join us during practise,' I asked.

She thought for a few seconds and said, 'Why not, I will get permission from my parents.'

'Great!' I said.

I remembered to leave the note on Ms Joseph's desk at the end of the day and Simran joined me on the field. I pushed her chair to where we were practising.

Today was the last day of practice, and tomorrow would be RACE DAY! Everyone gave it their best today. After we were all drained out of every ounce of energy and ready to pack up, I had a flash of an idea.

I ran to Mr Bolt before the girls' race started and begged him to allow me to take Simran for a run with the girls.

'Okay, but only once. I don't want anyone getting hurt,' he said.

'Thank you, thank you!' I said and ran to Simran.

'Where are you taking me?' she asked.

'I am going to make you run!' I said, pushing her chair to the start line.

'How Raghav? Are you crazy?' She was confused.

‘Quick, tie yourself up properly and we will compete against the girls,’ I said. ‘Hurry up!’

Simran was still puzzled at what I was up to, but fastened her seat belts.

Mr Bolt screamed, ‘Ready, steady, go!’

And I pushed Simran’s wheelchair on the track, while the other girls flew way past us. I pushed her with all my strength to roll her over to the finish line. I had thought it would be easy to push the wheelchair but it took all of my energy!

On the other hand, Simran was laughing out loud and clapping her hands. As she shouted out loud with delight, I forgot all about being tired.

We completed the race! We were the last ones but Simran was so excited, it didn’t matter.

‘Thanks, Raghav! You helped me run and not only that, it was the best run I have been on in a long time!’ she squeaked with excitement. ‘You are the best friend I have ever had!’

I wanted to tell Simran that I felt that way too! Ms Isha was right, I would find someone who would accept me with my difficulties.

'I hope you win the race tomorrow,' Simran said.

'I hope so too,' I said, as I crossed my fingers.

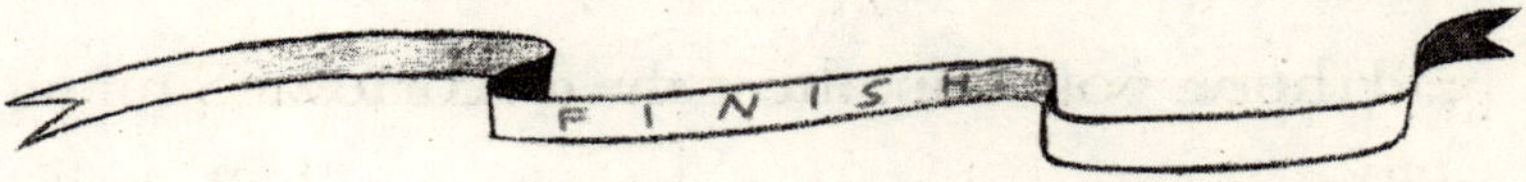

THE FINAL RACE

The end

Competing with a chance to win

TODAY WAS ATHLETICS DAY!
TODAY WAS RACE DAY!
TODAY WAS THE DAY I WAS GOING TO EITHER DO IT OR FAIL!

I was feeling electrified and nervous, both at the same time.

Electrified because I loved running. Every cell of my body was charged and nervous because I didn't know what would happen today. With Karan's extra practice, he was sure to win the gold medals.

But before the race began, we had half-day classes with Ms Joseph. It was going to be difficult to sit in class today with the race in the afternoon. All I could see were track lines and the finish line. My legs kept twitching as if I had no control over them.

'Raghav, you seem very thrilled. If given a choice, I am sure you would be out in the field now,' Ms Joseph joked.

I smiled and nodded my head excitedly.

'Please open to page seventy-three, we will do some reading today,' Ms Joseph announced.

'Popcorn reading?' Karan asked.

'Yes,' Ms Joseph said. 'Neetu, please begin.'

Neetu slowly stood up and started to read. This time I didn't want to miss a single word. Ms Isha had been working on my reading skills for a long time now. It had been difficult running through the same words over and over again with her, but I was learning a lot.

Ms Joseph called out to Daksh, then Vedh, Simran and Karan. I was hoping she would call my name but she didn't. I slowly raised my hand. 'Please could I read?'

'Are you sure, Raghav?' Ms Joseph asked.

I nodded.

'Go ahead,' she said.

I began.

'Scientists are res . . .' I struggled.

'Go on, Raghav,' Ms Joseph said, 'you are doing just fine.'

Karan looked at me and sighed, Daksh rolled his eyes, there was a sigh from Vedh too, but this time I didn't bother to worry and I read at my pace, which was slow but with less difficulties in reading. Simran helped me with the hard words. It was the first time ever, I had managed to read a paragraph without feeling nervous about reading.

'Very good, Raghav,' Ms Joseph said. 'I am so proud of the hard work you are putting in.'

Simran clapped her hands and everyone followed her, except Karan's gang. When everyone clapped, it lit a new spirit in me, and tears of a different kind stung my eyes. I ... I ... was overwhelmed as if I had won the most difficult race of my life! The road ahead may be long, but I had made the first step.

Ms Isha and Ms Joseph were the first two teachers who had said something nice about me. I knew this year and all the coming years of my school journey were going to be different. I felt the energy vibrating in my body. I was ready to step up to the starting line of the track. I wanted to RUN! I wanted to sprint! And this time, not away from anybody. Instead, I was ready to race towards the

no longer impossible task that Ms Joseph had made possible for me.

It was finally RACE time!

'Everybody, quickly warm up,' Mr Bolt shouted.

I did my jumps, stretches and tried to stay loose so that my legs wouldn't stiffen up. Mom, Papa and Shlok were sitting at the stands, waiting for the race to begin. Shlok had even made a board that said:

'GO SPRINTER GO'

I spotted Simran. When she saw me looking at her, she waved wildly to me and I waved back.

Mr Bolt blew the whistle and we lined up. I untied my lace and retied it tightly. Karan was all set, doing his jumps. My heart was thumping. Thump! Thump! Thump!

Mr Bolt blew the second whistle, signalling the time had come to begin our sprint to the finish line in a few seconds. I put my foot just before the start line, bent my body the way Mr Bolt had taught me and was ready for my leap forward.

The crowd cheered, and I took a few moments to scan the crowd. Shlok jumped high as he waved his sign. Mom and Papa gave me thumbs up signs and Simran squirmed in her chair with anticipation. The noise from the grandstands swelled as the clock ticked to the starting time. Out of nowhere, I heard Karan saying, 'I bet you have a disability to run too!' And he smirked.

I remembered what Ms Isha had said, 'People can be mean and unreasonable. It is best to IGNORE them.' With her words in my brain, that's precisely what I chose to do.

As I focused on the finish line, the cheers from the spectators, the chanting of the cheerleaders and Karan disappeared from my awareness. All the voices from the past that had haunted me, teased me and made fun of me vanished. My focus was directed on the red ribbon. I stretched my toes one last time inside my shoes.

Mr Bolt stepped up to the starting line and yelled, 'On your mark! Get set! GOOOOO!'

I went Boom.

I went Boom in the 50m.

I went Boom in the 100m.

And when I went Boom in the 200m, every nerve of my body pumped, my lungs desperately craved for air, my calf muscles stiffened. I kept telling myself to push harder! For a fraction of a second, I felt my heart would come out of my body and I would collapse, but I touched the finish line with Karan right behind me!

I went BOOM! BOOM! BOOM! And so did Shlok and Simran on seeing my gold medals.

Karan didn't look very happy. Vedh and Daksh tried to cheer him up. But that didn't work, as Karan kicked at a clump of grass and turned away from them.

'You ran well,' I said to Karan.

Karan kicked the grass again and rolled his eyes. Daksh and Vedh stuck to Karan and sulked like him, as if they had personally lost the gold medals.

This time Vedh's decision to stick to Karan and Daksh didn't bother me. I realized, Vedh had more things in common with Karan and Daksh. So maybe it was a good idea if they were together as friends.

I turned around and nearly tripped over Simran. She was right behind me.

'YAY! You WON!' She was jumping with excitement in her wheelchair, making me afraid that she was going to fall out of it.

Mom, Papa and Shlok were already making plans for celebrations with dinner at my favourite pizza place and they promised to top it off with double scoops of chocolate chip ice cream complete with sprinkles and whipped cream.

'Well done, Sprinter, you've aced it again!' Papa said.

'Way to go!' Mom said.

'You are the best!' Shlok said.

'Can we invite Simran to dinner with us?' I asked Mom and Papa.

'I see no reason why not, if her parents are okay with it,' Mom said.

'We can drop her home afterwards,' Papa said.

Simran's parents agreed instantly.

'Umm . . .' I looked at Papa. 'Please could you find out if the restaurant is wheelchair friendly?' I asked.

'That's very thoughtful of you, Raghav,' Papa said. 'I'll call them and find out.'

The restaurant WAS wheelchair friendly!

Shlok ordered his favourite small size all-cheese pizza and Mom and Papa decided to share a meal. Simran couldn't decide on her order.

'Do you want to share a pizza with me?' I offered.

'Thanks, Raghav, I was just hoping I'd find a partner to share a pizza with. I would never be able to finish a whole pizza.'

Everyone laughed at that.

We ordered a loaded veggie pizza with cheese and I cherished every bit of that evening and also the ice cream.

I was happy because I WON!

I was happy because I HAD FOUND A NEW FRIEND!

I was happy because I HAD NEVER BEEN SO HAPPY BEFORE!

ABOUT THE AUTHOR

Arti Sonthalia is crazzzyyy about books and stories. Her debut children's book *Big Bully and M-me* was nominated for the Crystal Kite Asia Award. *Hungry to Read* has touched many hearts and inspired even reluctant readers to read. Her next book *Best Friends Forever* has won the FICCI Book of the Year Award in 2020. Sonthalia's *Hungry to Play* was shortlisted for the Neev Book Awards 2020.

If you meet Sonthalia over a cup of coffee, she can talk non-stop about a good book. She has also been a TEDx speaker. When not writing, she is busy listening to music and reading. Sonthalia loves long walks and enjoys chocolates too!